Thanks to the Animals

Allen Sockabasin
Passamaquoddy Storyteller

Illustrated by
Rebekah Raye

Tilbury House, Publishers
Thomaston, Maine

Winter had arrived.
Joo Tum worked for days preparing
for the trip north with his family.

He took apart their house near the shore
and stacked the cedar logs on the big bobsled.

Everyone helped.

They packed the family sled
   with his tools and with the meats and fish and vegetables
     harvested during the summer, when the days were long.

It was loaded to the very top with precious food,
but Joo Tum made sure there was room
for his children to ride in the back.

Everyone dressed in warm sealskin clothes
for the long trip.
It was time to go to their winter home
in the deep woods.
The horses pulled the sled slowly through the new snow.

Zoo Sap was not yet walking,
        but he was a strong baby, born in the spring.
He rode on the sled with the other children.

As the shadows grew long, the older children slept.
But then little Zoo Sap stood up and tumbled off the sled!

Oh, how Zoo Sap cried! His voice filled the sky.

The animals of the forest were alerted by his crying.
First to come were the beaver.
    They knew they had to keep him warm and dry,
        so they put their tails together and cradled Zoo Sap.

Zoo Sap still cried, so the moose came.
Then the bear, the caribou, and the deer.
The fox and the wolf came, too.
And all the big animals lay together in a circle.

Then the other, smaller animals came—
    the raccoons, porcupines, rabbits, weasels, and mink.
        The muskrat and otter and the squirrels and mice came, too.

They gathered and filled in the cracks
between the big animals.
At sunset the owl came.

Then the raven, crow, jay, duck, and a goose
gathered to perch on top.

Even a seagull came.

Last came the great bald eagle,
who spread her wings over all the other birds and animals.
Zoo Sap stayed warm.

When Joo Tum arrived at his winter home
he knew something was very wrong.

Zoo Sap was missing.

Joo Tum quickly lit a fire for his family
    and got them settled.
            Then he turned back to the trail to find his son.

He traveled through the woods all night,
and just at sunrise he came to a big mound of snow.
Resting on top was the great bald eagle.

"I knew you would come back for Zoo Sap," the eagle said.
Joo Tum looked down and saw his son,
safely sleeping in a great pile of warm animals.

Joo Tum thanked the animals one by one.
Then he took Zoo Sap in his strong arms
and went back to the family.

When they arrived that evening,
there was feasting and dancing.

What a celebration!

Author's Note

You may wonder why the family in this story takes down their cabin and moves to a different place. The reason has to do with the seasonal migrations my people once made.

The natural world was a great gift to the Passamaquoddy people from our Creator. For thousands of years we roamed vast lands for our livelihood and our traditional way of life. My people freely migrated over these lands, especially along the waterways, moving with the changes of seasons and as our physical and social needs dictated. The lands and waters provided a diversity and abundance of resources to sustain us. Our migrations also helped to maintain a good ecological balance without depleting any one area of its resources.

The stories of how we migrated with the seasons between salt water shores and the marshlands and deep woods have been passed down from our ancestors through many generations of oral tradition. How far back do the stories go? Since they are not written history, we do not know, but we know they come from long ago. (The Passamaquoddy word for "long ago" sounds like *be-chah*, with the accent on the second syllable.)

In spring, summer, and early fall, coastal shores provided an open and cool climate as well as access to fish, shellfish, and berries to gather. When the pollack and cod were running, whole families would travel to the fishing grounds to smoke and dry fish for several weeks. ("Passamaquoddy" is our word for pollack; we are the people of the pollack.) They would also hunt porpoise for meat—a main staple for our people—and for oil to light our lamps.

The migration inland usually started in the fall and with the early snows. The woodland regions provided shelter from winter winds, which blow fierce and bitter over the open coastal barrens. The deep woods provided firewood as well as natural habitat for big game such as deer and moose, and the marshlands bordering ponds and the inland reaches of estuaries provided habitat for beaver, mink, otter, and

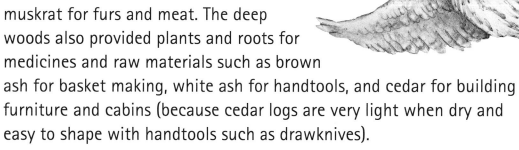

muskrat for furs and meat. The deep woods also provided plants and roots for medicines and raw materials such as brown ash for basket making, white ash for handtools, and cedar for building furniture and cabins (because cedar logs are very light when dry and easy to shape with handtools such as drawknives).

Our coastal lands began to narrow as settlements of non-native people grew and the concept of land ownership was introduced. Our migrations become more contained and focused in smaller regions, and we began to settle and band in small groups and villages, fearing the loss of the land that had sustained us for many generations.

Once we acquired horses through trade with other settlers, we were able to move our households and even our cabins on huge sleds made of white ash and maple. My grandfather and my dad made sleds and log cabins from cedar logs that were cut by hand and without nails. The logs were fitted exactly to each other using hardwood pegs, and they could be assembled and disassembled over and over. Cedar shakes were used for the roofs.

Over the years, we lived more of each year in the woods as our access to coastal lands dwindled. Using horses, we were able to clear lands near our cabins to plant gardens to supplement our hunting and trapping. We "settled" a portion of the land over which we had roamed for generations. Our principal settlement is today known as the village "upriver."

Thanks to the Animals is a story of a transitional time for the Passamaquoddy people. The family in the story has horses but is still migrating away from the coast and into the woods as the first snows fall. The story is also just what it says—an offering of thanks to the animals that sustained our people through the generations.

—Allen Sockabasin

The Passamaquoddy language is still spoken by many members of the tribe, and there are ongoing efforts to increase the number of tribal children who speak their native language. Once, the Passamaquoddy and related tribes occupied lands between Maine and New Brunswick, Canada. Today there are approximately 3,200 tribal members, and the tribe owns 142,000 acres of land in Maine, which it monitors and maintains. Many Passamaquoddy live at Zee-byig (Pleasant Point) on Passamaquoddy Bay, or at Mud-doc-mig-goog (Indian Township) near the St. Croix River.

Below are Passamaquoddy names for the animals in this book, spelled phonetically by Allen to help English-speaking people become familiar with the Passamaquoddy language as it has been spoken traditionally.

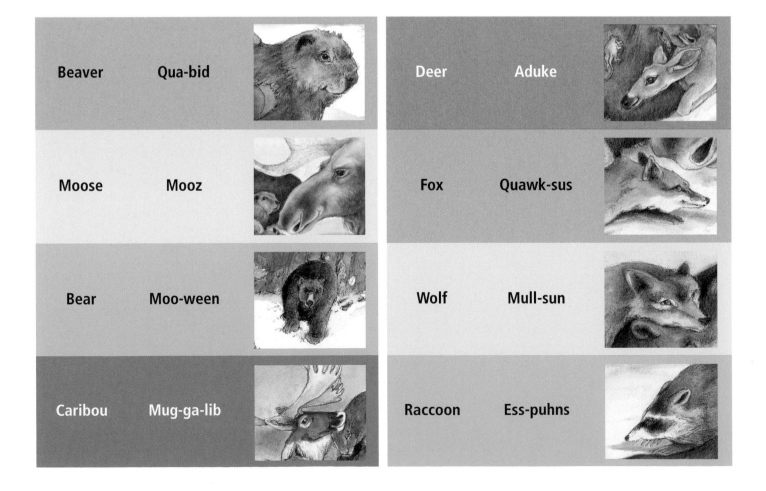

Beaver	Qua-bid		Deer	Aduke
Moose	Mooz		Fox	Quawk-sus
Bear	Moo-ween		Wolf	Mull-sun
Caribou	Mug-ga-lib		Raccoon	Ess-puhns

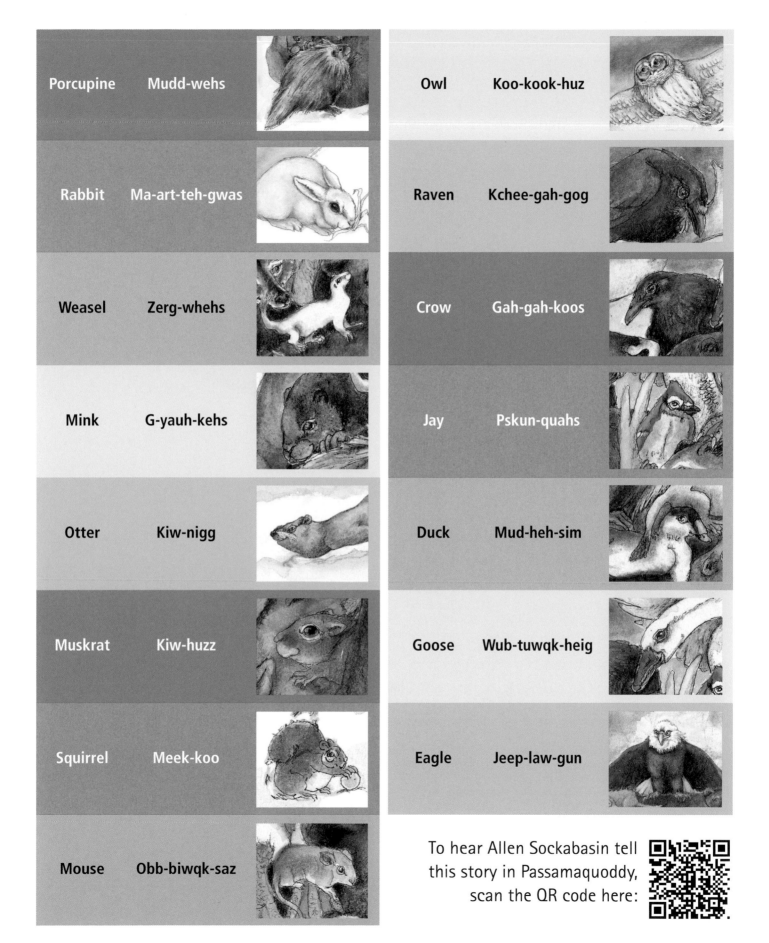

Porcupine	Mudd-wehs	
Rabbit	Ma-art-teh-gwas	
Weasel	Zerg-whehs	
Mink	G-yauh-kehs	
Otter	Kiw-nigg	
Muskrat	Kiw-huzz	
Squirrel	Meek-koo	
Mouse	Obb-biwqk-saz	

Owl	Koo-kook-huz	
Raven	Kchee-gah-gog	
Crow	Gah-gah-koos	
Jay	Pskun-quahs	
Duck	Mud-heh-sim	
Goose	Wub-tuwqk-heig	
Eagle	Jeep-law-gun	

To hear Allen Sockabasin tell this story in Passamaquoddy, scan the QR code here:

Dedications:

This book is dedicated to my mom, Molly Zoo-Sap,
for many of my stories. —AJS

To Kenny for his love and thoughtful understanding,
and for my family. —RR

Tilbury House, Publishers
12 Starr Street
Thomaston, Maine 04861
800-582-1899 • www.tilburyhouse.com

First hardcover printing, July 2005 • Second edition, first hardcover printing, 2014
18 17   WOR   5 4 3

ISBN 978-0-88448-414-1

Library of Congress Cataloging-in-Publication Data for the First Edition
Sockabasin, Allen, 1944-
  Thanks to the Animals / by Allen Sockabasin ; illustrated by Rebekah Raye.
    p. cm.
Summary: In 1900 during the Passamaquoddy winter migration in Maine, Baby Zoo Sap falls off the family bobsled and the forest animals hearing his cries, gather to protect him until his father returns to find him.
  ISBN 978-0-88448-270-3 (hardcover : alk. paper)
 [1. Babies--Fiction. 2. Forest animals--Fiction. 3. Passamaquoddy Indians--Fiction. 4. Indians of North America--Maine--Fiction. 5. Maine--History--20th century--Fiction. I. Raye, Rebekah, ill. II. Title.
  PZ7.S685252Th 2005
  [E]--dc22
                              2004029039

Printed by Worzalla, Stevens Point, Wisconsin